AF407956

BEN KOOL
OF
CONLEY RANCH

DENNIS H. WILLIAMS

For information contact: info@outlawspublishing.com
Editor Michael Clement
Cover Art by Eva Lee Williams
Cover design by Outlaws Publishing.
Published by Outlaws Publishing.
January 2025
10 9 8 7 6 5 4 3 2 1

Chapter One

The cold January wind swept across the southwest Sonoran Desert, its icy fingers bending the resilient greasewood bushes into unnatural arcs. The Palo Verde trees groaned and creaked under the force, their thin branches popping like distant gunfire in the stillness of the night. Beneath the faint starlight, Dead Horse Tank lay cloaked in shadow, its usually tranquil surface rippled by the relentless gusts.

A small fire flickered and danced within a makeshift camp on the bank, casting wavering shadows against the canvas of a weathered tent. The tent flap was half-open, inviting warmth from the fire but revealing little of its occupant. Inside, Ben Kool lay beneath a tattered blanket, his rugged face illuminated faintly by the firelight. His hand rested out of sight beneath the covers, fingers brushing the cold steel grip of a pistol.

The low rumble of an approaching engine cut through the wind, then ceased abruptly. Moments later, the sharp slam of a car door echoed through the night. Ben tensed. His fingers curled tighter around the pistol as he listened intently. Footsteps crunched on the gravel, and a shadow emerged from the darkness to stand just within the fire's glow.

"You're a hard man to find, Ben." The voice was calm and familiar, belonging to a tall black man dressed in a heavy coat. He held up a large manila envelope. "I brought something for you—from the boss."

Ben's eyes narrowed; his face shadowed with suspicion. "I didn't want to be found, Jason. And I don't want anything from the boss." His voice was low but firm, with a hint of exhaustion. "I quit two weeks ago, and I meant it. Seven years of having my pucker string pulled tight was enough. All I need is the confirmation slip for the last deposit to my bank account."

Jason sighed, stepping closer to the fire's warmth. He opened the envelope and sifted through its contents, finally pulling out a crisp white slip of paper. "Here's the confirmation slip," he said, extending it toward Ben.

Ben slowly sat up, his blanket slipping to his waist. He took the slip, scanned it, then slid it into his shirt pocket. Jason wasn't finished. "There's something else I think you need to see," he said, pulling a folded yellow poster from the envelope. "Whether you go back or not."

Ben unfolded the poster, his breath catching as his eyes took in the bold print: a wanted notice offering twenty thousand dollars for his head. The bounty, issued from Beirut, promised payment upon delivery—his head alone.

Ben's jaw tightened. "I knew this was coming," he muttered. "I just didn't think it'd be that much."

Jason stepped closer, his expression unreadable. "That's a lot of money, Ben. And there are people in this country who wouldn't think twice about collecting."

Ben exhaled sharply and his breath was visible in the cold air. "My life wouldn't be worth a plug nickel if I went back to the company. I've got a good nest egg, and I'm done. I want my life back the way it used to be." He paused, staring into the fire. "My answer is still no, Jason. And for both our sakes, forget where you found me. I'm out."

Jason nodded, his eyes lingering on Ben for a moment. "Okay, Ben. Have a good life. But watch your back. Taliban operatives are here, and with that kind of bounty on your head, someone's bound to come looking. I don't wanna read your name in the obituaries."

He turned and walked back into the darkness. The crunch of his boots on the gravel grew faint, and soon the sound of an engine roared to life. Moments later, Jason's car disappeared into the distance, leaving Dead Horse Tank in silence once more.

Ben tossed another piece of ironwood onto the fire, watching as the flames surged and hissed. He pulled the blanket tightly around himself, leaning back against his pack. His voice was barely audible over the wind as he muttered to himself, "Tomorrow, we start anew."

Above, the stars bore silent witness to his resolve, twinkling faintly through the encroaching desert clouds.

Chapter Two

The Salt River National Bank bustled with quiet activity as customers streamed in and out through the double glass doors. Jim Caldwell, the vice president, sat at his desk near the back of the main floor. His well-practiced hobby of watching people was interrupted by the arrival of a man who immediately stood out.

The man wore a black Resistol hat, a white pearl snap shirt, and freshly starched Wrangler jeans. His dark aviator glasses obscured his eyes, and his polished brown Olathe boots gave him an air of quiet authority. As he lingered just inside the doorway, Caldwell decided to make the first move, striding across the room and extending his hand.

"Can I help you with something? I'm Jim Caldwell, the vice president of the bank."

The stranger's voice was calm but firm. "Are you the one who handles bank properties? The foreclosed ones?"

"I can do that. Are you interested in one, Mister...?" Caldwell's polished smile faltered slightly as the man released his handshake.

"Ben Kool," he replied. "I'm interested in the old Conley Ranch, east and south of Gila Bend."

Caldwell led Kool to his desk and pulled up the property details on his computer. "Here it is. The Conley Ranch is 160 acres of deeded land, plus 20 acres around Javelina Well. The grazing lease permits 200 head across a hundred sections. The bank's asking price is $275,000. That includes the registered brand. The property is vacant and ready for immediate occupancy."

"I'll pay $175,000 today," Ben said flatly, meeting Caldwell's eyes with a piercing stare.

Caldwell hesitated, visibly thrown. "That's a hundred-thousand-dollar discount. I don't think we can do that."

"Get your boss," Ben replied coolly.

Moments later, Caldwell returned with Mister Anderson, the bank's white-haired president.

"Mister Kool, we're not in the business of discounting property," Anderson began firmly.

"You will discount this one," Ben countered. "The property's been mismanaged for two years. The corrals are gone—used for firewood. The wells have been stripped of pumping equipment. The house is vandalized to the point of needing a rebuild. You took all the cattle and didn't apply it to the loan. My offer stands: $175,000."

Anderson and Caldwell stepped aside, whispering hurriedly. When they returned, Anderson straightened his posture.

"How much of a down payment will you make, and how many years to pay off the balance?"

Ben's tone was resolute. "It's a cash offer. I'll take a quitclaim deed for the deeded property today and expect the grazing leases when they record."

Pulling out a folded checkbook, Ben wrote a check and handed it to Caldwell. The vice president typed the account number into his computer, his eyes widening as the account balance appeared.

"Will you keep your account with us after the transaction?" Caldwell ventured.

"If we finish, yes. If not, I'll move it," Ben replied.

Anderson, having glimpsed the screen, clapped Caldwell on the shoulder. "We'll finish this right now. Nice doing business with you, Mister Kool."

An hour later, Ben exited the bank with a manila folder containing the quitclaim deed and a receipt for his check. Standing on the sidewalk, he took a deep breath.

"Well, that wasn't too bad, was it?" he said to himself, striding toward the parking lot.

He climbed into a faded blue Dodge Power Wagon, started the Cummins diesel engine, and headed south, the sun glinting off the windshield as he drove toward a new chapter of his life.

Chapter Three

Later that evening, Ben sat in a corner booth at Mi Sombrero Mexican Restaurant, the warm smell of grilled meats and fresh tortillas filling the air. Across from him, B.J. Grant, an old friend and the town's Justice of the Peace, sipped from a frosted Dos Equis bottle. They'd grown up together, attending the same schools from first grade through high school.

"I think you're off your rocker, Ben," B.J. said, shaking his head. "Two hundred cows on that desert land won't make you a dime."

"Delson Conley managed it for years," Ben replied, spearing a slice of carne asada with his fork. "Besides, I don't need to make a living off it—just supplement what I've already got. If it rains, I'll contract some steers, too." He popped the steak into his mouth, savoring the smoky flavor.

"But you've got to rebuild everything out there," B.J. nearly yelled, leaning forward.

"I know." Ben's voice was steady, but his eyes darkened. "I spent two weeks going over the place. I've seen her dirty laundry—nothing's hidden. I can do it, B.J.

I want a home, not just a place to stay. The rest will be gravy."

B.J. leaned back, staring at Ben. "You're serious about this, huh?"

Ben nodded, his expression softening for a moment. "I've spent ten years traveling the world, doing dirty jobs for the government. My mind's cluttered with memories I'll never shake, but maybe... maybe I can quiet them for a while. This place feels like it could be my peace."

B.J. sighed and took another swig of his beer. "All right, it's your money. What do you need from me?"

"A handy man—a good one," Ben said, setting his fork down. "Someone who knows carpentry and plumbing. I've got a solar well company coming tomorrow to install a tank and panels at the house. Whoever you send needs to be ready to work. I'll pay well."

A grin spread across B.J.'s face. "I've got just the guy: Rattlesnake Dan. He's a Vietnam vet, tough as nails, and makes hatbands from rattlesnake hides when he's not working odd jobs. He's been on a month-long bender, so he could use some drying out."

Ben chuckled, shaking his head. "Sounds like a character. Send him out in the morning. He can camp at the house while he works. If he has a helper, he can bring him along. I've already got the Morales brothers lined up to rebuild the corrals and fix up the barn. It's time to stir up some dust." He brought his fist down on the table, making the glasses rattle.

B.J. laughed. "Well, no one's run cattle on that land in two years, so you've got time before you wear it out—if it rains."

Ben leaned forward, a sly grin creeping across his face. "There's cattle there already, B.J.—along the south fence, next to Jeff Hardisty's spread. Their tracks are deep, a foot in places. Whoever gathered for the bank left plenty behind." He chuckled. "That banker doesn't even know it. They're watering at the old gun site well."

B.J. whistled low. "Figures. That outfit the bank hired couldn't find their own boots if they were on fire. You've got an edge, then, but it's still a gamble."

Ben's grin faded, and his tone turned serious. "I've been gone a decade, but I haven't forgotten what Delson taught me. I'll make it work."

B.J. drained his beer and stood. "All right, but when you go belly up, I'll let you crash at my place. See you, Ben."

Ben watched his friend stroll out, shaking his head with a smile. Picking up the check, he walked to the register. As he paid, he thought, *"I'll sleep in my own house. This time, no one's running me off."*

Chapter Four

A month after Rattlesnake Dan began restoring the ranch house at the old Conley Ranch, Ben Kool finally moved in. The place wasn't perfect yet—Dan was still finishing up the porch—but the essentials were in place. A propane refrigerator and stove hummed softly in the kitchen, and a wood-burning stove promised warmth when the desert nights turned cold.

Ben spent his evenings on the porch, sprawled in an old easy chair he'd dragged outside, a tall glass of bourbon resting on the small table beside him. The horizon blazed in hues of orange and pink as the sun sank below the mountains, and for the first time in years, he felt something like peace.

He'd made progress in more ways than one. With the money he'd sunk into the ranch, he'd bought four sturdy, desert-bred horses and a stock trailer. The days were spent riding the far reaches of the ranch, reacquainting himself with the land he now called home. At the gun site, the Morales brothers had constructed a sturdy corral, complete with triggers to trap the cattle that came to water. Ben had scattered salt blocks in strategic spots, drawing the animals out of the brush, and their tracks showed he'd chosen wisely.

The time was nearing to set the triggers and see just what kind of "boogers" roamed the area. Still, every day of riding helped ease the weight he carried—memories of distant places, of violence, and of decisions that would never leave him. Yet, when it came to leaving his pistol behind on those rides, he couldn't quite bring himself to do it. The wanted poster still lingered in the back of his mind, a shadow that refused to fade entirely.

One evening, as the first stars pricked the darkening sky, Ben sat on the porch, sorting through the stack of mail B.J. had brought out earlier. Most of it was junk, but his bank statement caught his eye. Opening the envelope, he leaned forward in his chair. The numbers on the page hit him harder than he'd expected.

The day he'd bought the ranch, there had been $879,000 in his account—a decade of hard-earned pay from jobs he'd rather forget. Now, the balance had dwindled to less than $150,000.

Ben leaned back, cradling his bourbon, and stared out at the shadowed expanse of his land. He owned the ranch outright now, no debt hanging over his head. The house was almost new, the fixtures and infrastructure rebuilt from the ground up. The barn stood sturdy, the corrals ready for use, and the wells were operational. Yet, the question loomed: how many cattle were still out there?

He'd seen their trails—deep, well-worn grooves carved into the land—and had caught glimpses of small herds in the distance. From what he could tell, they were good stock, hardy animals with plenty of Brahma blood to endure the desert's harshness. But the coming heat would make working them dangerous. Stressing the cattle in the sweltering months could mean losing weight or even lives.

Ben swirled the amber liquid in his glass, thinking. He'd need to gather and sell a few head soon to pad his dwindling bank account, but it required careful planning. Tomorrow, he'd start putting a plan together.

For now, though, he let himself sink back into the chair, the evening's stillness wrapping around him. The bourbon warmed his throat as he watched the last light fade from the sky, dreaming of quieter days that always seemed just out of reach.

Chapter Five

While Ben Kool planned his next move to round up the remnants of cattle on his ranch, banker Anderson and Jim Caldwell were crafting plans of their own.

As the last bank employee and customer exited the building, Caldwell locked the double glass doors behind them. He returned to his desk, gathered a stack of papers, and walked into Anderson's office. Anderson, seated behind his oak desk, had poured two glasses of Royal Crown whiskey. The amber liquid glistened in the dim light.

Caldwell licked his lips as he handed over the papers and picked up his drink. Taking a long pull, he sighed with satisfaction. Anderson barely glanced at the stack in Caldwell's hand.

"Don't make me read all this, Jim," Anderson said, leaning back in his swivel chair and swirling the whiskey in his glass. "Just tell me what you found out."

"Well," Caldwell began, settling into a chair opposite Anderson, "Kool was born and raised in Gila Bend. His mother ran off when he was three, and his father worked as a section superintendent for Southern Pacific. In high school, Kool was a three-letter athlete and earned decent grades, but his father died of cancer during his junior year. He didn't have any other family, so Delson Conley took him in until he graduated."

Anderson sipped his whiskey as Caldwell continued. "After that, Kool joined the Army. His Department of Defense record shows he moved up the ranks quickly, eventually becoming a sergeant in the Special Forces, specializing in weapons training. His last year in the service was spent in Beirut. Then, after his discharge... nothing. For seven years, there's no public trace of him until he walked into this bank."

Caldwell took another long drink, draining his glass, before leaning forward. "Here's the interesting part. That account he opened? It was funded by DYNA CORP, a Pentagon contractor. They handle jobs the military can't officially touch. Every year for seven years, they deposited $150,000 into his account—tax-free. Kool never touched a dime of it until the day he walked in here. Since then, though, he's been spending heavily. Rebuilding the ranch, I'd imagine."

Anderson's brow furrowed as he poured another round for them both. "Have we heard from the mules down in Caborca since Kool bought the ranch?"

"No," Caldwell replied, reaching for his refill. "The cartel's been holding off sending mules through that corridor, and now it's getting too hot for them to haul cargo through the desert."

Anderson leaned back, his chair creaking slightly. "If we hadn't sold Kool that ranch, the Board of Directors would've been asking all kinds of questions. We'll just have to wait and see what happens in the next few months. If it gets messy, we might have to send him the same way Conley went."

Anderson's tone darkened. "If Kool ever finds out there wasn't a loan on that ranch and that the cartel's been using it as a corridor, we won't see the light of day."

Caldwell smirked and reached into his jacket pocket. "This might solve our problem." He unfolded a worn wanted poster and laid it on Anderson's desk.

Anderson leaned forward, studying the poster carefully. His eyes narrowed as he read it a second time. "Do the Taliban know where Kool is?"

"I don't know," Caldwell said, his grin widening, "but I'll make sure the cartel does. They'll pass it along. That's where a lot of their product ends up anyway."

Anderson set his glass down, the faint clink echoing in the room. "Make it so. They've got five months to clean it up. Once that's done, we'll take possession of the ranch, just like we did when Conley died. Start prepping the paperwork—we'll need it ready to file."

Caldwell's grin spread even wider as Anderson's gaze turned distant, focused on the dollar signs dancing in his head.

Chapter Six

The Gun-Site Well wasn't named for the ghost town in the mountains, though nobody knew its true origin. The country around it was a maze of washes and arroyos, the land cut deeply and shaped by time. Each dry streambed was lined with a forest of mesquite, palo verde, and the occasional ironwood tree, their branches casting spindly shadows in the harsh desert sun.

The Morales brothers had built a sturdy set of corrals here, modeled after the shipping pens of the Southern Pacific Railroad. Railroad ties stood side by side with a precise two-inch gap between each, their weathered surfaces rough to the touch. A thick, one-inch cable ran around the top, tensioned by turnbuckles to keep the fence upright under pressure. A heavy, fourteen-foot pipe gate marked one corner, and in the middle of the fence line, a set of durable triggers allowed for sorting cattle. Along one side of the corral, an alleyway had been constructed, perfect for organizing and loading livestock into trailers.

Nearby, the windmill had been repaired, its new leathers ensuring a steady gush of water from the pipe into the concrete storage tank, now full to overflowing. Ben Kool made a point of keeping salt blocks in the corral at all times, knowing the cattle relied on them.

The morning sun had barely risen when Ben rode out to the corrals, leaving his truck and trailer parked a good two miles away to avoid disturbing the cattle. What he found took him by surprise: the corral was teeming with cattle of all sizes and ages. Long-eared Brahmas pressed together, their slick hides shimmering in the early light.

Sitting astride his horse, Ben leaned over the fence to count the cattle. It wasn't long before he realized he was outmatched. The numbers far exceeded what he could handle alone. His attention was drawn southward by a low, mournful bawl. Another string of cattle meandered toward the well, drawn by the promise of water.

A deep frown settled on Ben's face. The land couldn't sustain this many cattle. Overgrazing would destroy it, and the consequences for the herd could be devastating. He'd need help to sort and relocate them across the ranch.

Among the cattle, Ben spotted three massive, gray Brahma bulls bearing the Conley brand. Most of the cows were marked, but there were unbranded heifers and young bulls scattered throughout. He dismounted and eased through the gate, careful not to spook the herd. Methodically, he opened the gate to the alley, ensuring the out-gate was latched, and began sorting. The three branded bulls were his focus. They moved reluctantly under his quiet pressure, their heavy bodies lumbering into the alley.

It took a good half-hour to separate them from the rest of the herd. Ben wiped the sweat from his brow as he finished, a satisfied nod marking his accomplishment. Mounting his horse, he loped back to the truck and trailer.

Backing the trailer up to the alley gate, he unloaded his horse, then coaxed the bulls into the trailer. They climbed in without protest, their docility a welcome surprise. Ben secured the gates and loaded his horse behind them, the metal clanging loudly in the quiet desert air.

By the time he reached the headquarters corrals, the sun was high in the sky, its heat beating relentlessly down. Ben unloaded the bulls, settling them into a shaded pen, and turned his horse loose. The day's work wasn't over, but his mind was already turning to the evening.

After securing the ranch, he drove into town. The scent of sizzling steak greeted him as he stepped into the diner, his stomach growling in response. Over supper, he spoke with several ranch hands, laying out his plans and gauging their interest in helping the next day.

The work ahead was daunting. He calculated at least four or five trailer loads to move the cattle to the main corrals, and from there, many would need to be relocated to other parts of the ranch. The Gun-Site Well corrals were overburdened, and the land couldn't bear the strain.

As Ben finished his meal and paid his tab, a ranch hand leaned in conspiratorially. "You've got your hands full, Kool. Better watch your back out there."

Ben's expression remained neutral, but the words lingered as he left the diner. The night air was cooler now, but the tension in his chest felt heavier than before. Tomorrow would be a long day, and he couldn't shake the feeling that trouble was brewing on the horizon.

Chapter Seven

The drive to town gave Ben Kool plenty of time to mull over the cattle situation. The numbers left behind by the bank were staggering—far more than the ranch could sustain without careful management. He decided it was time to make some changes. The Brahma blood in his herd had its advantages, but he figured it was time to bring in some English breeding. Younger bulls, maybe Herefords, would give him the balance he needed.

As for the cows, he had more than enough. Ben resolved to sell off some of the older stock, including a few straight gray humpy cows that Delson Conley had been so fond of. Delson had sworn by those cows, believing in their resilience, but Ben knew the modern market required something different. The Sonoran Desert demanded hardy cattle, but too much Brahma blood wasn't the answer.

These thoughts churned through his mind as he reached the outskirts of Gila Bend. The familiar sight of Mi Sombrero, a local diner with sun-faded paint and a neon sombrero sign, made his stomach growl. Ben parked the truck and stepped inside, the smell of grilled meat and roasted chiles a welcome comfort. He ordered a meal and a beer, settling into a corner booth where he could keep an eye on the street.

While waiting for his food, Ben noticed a pickup with stock racks parked across the way. The vehicle had the well-worn, dust-covered look of a working man's truck. His curiosity got the better of him, and when the waitress brought his meal, he gestured toward the truck.

"Who drives that rig over there?" he asked.

The waitress, a middle-aged woman with sharp eyes and a kind smile, nodded toward a booth two rows down. "That's Clifford Barnes. You want to talk to him?"

"Bring me his check, then tell him I'd like a word," Ben replied, taking a bite of his enchilada.

When Clifford had finished his meal, he got up and walked over. The man was weathered, his face etched with lines from years spent under the Arizona sun. His hat was battered, and his boots were well-worn but clean, tell-tale signs of a man who took pride in his work. With one glance, Ben knew this was a real cattleman.

"Sit down," Ben said, nodding toward the empty seat across from him. "Can I buy you a beer?"

"I don't drink anymore, but I'll have a Coke if you don't mind," Clifford replied, his voice carrying a faint wheeze.

"You wanted to talk to me?"

"I bought the Conley Outfit. I need help for a few days. Would you be available?" Ben explained.

"You would be Ben Kool then," Clifford said, settling into the booth. "Dan told me about you. I knew Delson pretty well. I don't believe for a second that he drank himself to death, but that's another story. Yes, I can help you for a few days. My work's caught up. When do we start?"

"First thing in the morning," Ben replied. "I've got a corral full of unbranded mavericks and calves that need working and moving to the house. We could use another man if you know of one."

Clifford nodded thoughtfully, pulling a cigarette from his shirt pocket but leaving it unlit. "I'll see what I can do. What time in the morning?"

"Be there around 5:30 or 6:00," Ben said, cutting into his steak. "I'll have breakfast ready. Bring a couple of horses—I'll feed them while you're there. Most of the work will be hauling, sorting, and corral work."

Clifford stood and extended a calloused hand. "It's good to meet ya. Dan said you were a straight-up kind of fella. I'll be there in the morning."

Ben shook his hand firmly. "I'll see you then."

As Clifford walked out the door, the waitress came by with a fresh beer for Ben. She leaned on the edge of the booth, her smile amused. "I've known him ten years, and that's the most I've ever heard him talk."

Ben chuckled, raising his beer in acknowledgment.

She continued, "Clifford's got a greasy sack outfit on the road to Ajo. Comes in once a week or so. Good, honest cowboy—always has been."

That was all Ben needed to hear. As he finished his meal, his thoughts shifted from plans to action. Tomorrow would bring a full day's work, but with Clifford on his side, he felt a glimmer of confidence.

Chapter Eight

The first morning, Ben and Clifford pulled up to the corrals at Gun-site. Ben almost choked at the sight. The corral was so full that the cattle could hardly move. More had come through the triggers during the night to get a drink. Ben backed the trailer up to the alley gate as Clifford used his horse to work the herd, loosening them up.

After half an hour of careful maneuvering, Clifford managed to slip a trailer load into the alley—mostly cull cows, a couple of old bulls, and a few mavericks. Once loaded, Ben drove back to the main corrals at the headquarters. While he was gone, Clifford kept sorting, getting cattle into the alley that Ben would keep—cows with little calves and middle-aged cows.

In an hour, he had the alley full again. Opening the gate, he let the cattle back out to graze. Then the process was repeated until the main corral had room again. Clifford began sorting the cull cows, bulls, and mavericks for the next load when Ben returned.

By the second day, the two men had cleaned up the bunch at the Gun-site corrals. The corrals at the house now held two truckloads of cattle. Ben and Clifford sat on the porch, sipping cold drinks in the late afternoon heat.

Clifford, silent for a moment, finally spoke up. "I told you I didn't believe Delson drank himself to death. When they found him in his truck, he smelled to high heaven of booze. The coroner said he died of alcohol poisoning. I didn't believe it then, and I still don't know. He took a drink from time to time, but I never, in twenty years, saw him drunk. I'm telling you this because it's haunted me for two long years."

Ben turned to look at Clifford. "Do you think it was murder?"

"I don't know what to think," Clifford said, shaking his head. "But that wasn't how Delson was. The week before, he found a trail of illegals crossing the ranch, and he was mad about it. Maybe that had something to do with it. I just don't know."

Clifford leaned back in his chair, staring off into the distance. "Well, we can't do much about it right now. Can you send those Morales boys out in the morning? We could use them when we brand all those mavericks."

Ben nodded thoughtfully. "I'm going to keep about forty head of the best heifers and put them down at Javelina Well, but we'll still be overstocked. Next fall, we'll cull deeper to get us closer to the permit."

Ben was rambling, his mind occupied with the story Clifford had shared about Delson. The weight of it hung heavily, but the work of the ranch demanded focus.

Chapter Nine

The truck driver, Leonard Hazelbaker, rolled down the door on the cattle truck after the last cow had loaded. The brand inspector, who had been standing next to the chute, handed him a handful of papers. Leonard glanced at Ben, "Marana sale barn, right?"

Ben nodded. "I won't be far behind you. I want to be there for the sale tomorrow. Be sure they put them on feed and water right away."

Leonard nodded, climbed into the cab of his idling truck, and pulled out.

The brand inspector approached where Ben and Clifford sat on their horses. "You said there's still a bunch of cattle left here? I heard the bank cleaned this outfit out when Mister Conley died."

"That's what we were told, but I'm starting to wonder," Ben answered, frowning. He turned to Clifford. "Do you know who gathered the cattle for the bank?"

"I didn't know a thing about it until after it was all over. I think it's kinda funny." Clifford glanced at the brand inspector. "Can you check and see who inspected the cattle and how many there were? There ought to be a record somewhere."

"I'll look into it and let you know. It all happened before I got transferred here from Flagstaff," the inspector replied as he walked back toward his truck. "See you in a few days." He waved as he drove off.

Ben reached into his shirt pocket and pulled out a folded check, handing it to Clifford. "Thanks. I know you helping here put you in a bind at home."

"Naw, but if I get a fresh horse, I'll catch up quick." Clifford smiled, stuffing the check into his shirt pocket. He walked over to his truck, jumped his horse into the back, and shut the gate. "Give me a holler if ya need something." He waved as he got in his truck and drove off.

Ben headed into the house to clean up. As he stepped into the shower, he heard a car door slam. He pulled back the curtain and heard Rattlesnake Dan holler, "I'll be out in a minute! Get a cold drink and make yourself at home."

"Done!" Ben yelled back.

When Ben came out, buttoning his shirt, Dan was sitting on the porch with a cold beer in hand. "Hey, can I prowl around for some snakes?"

"I'll do better than that," Ben said with a grin. "You can stay here tonight and tomorrow, do the chores, and keep the varmints from packing the place out. I'll pay you. You can have every damn snake you find."

"Deal!" Dan jumped up and headed for his truck. He pulled a bed roll from the back and threw it on the porch. "I'm your man."

Chapter Ten

The day after the Marana sale, Ben was preparing to head home to the ranch. His cattle had been sold at a fair price, but not the top price. He had noticed that the top-selling cattle didn't carry as much Brahma blood. He had contacted a Hereford breeder and arranged for 15 head of Hereford bulls to be delivered to the ranch. He figured if he pushed hard and rode straight, he'd be home by 11:00 or 12:00 that morning.

Meanwhile, Dan had woken up early in the predawn darkness, wrapped in his bedroll on the Conley ranch porch. He had gotten up, rolled his bed, and placed it out of the way, then went inside the house for a breakfast meal and coffee before starting the morning chores. After eating, he lingered over another cup of coffee, waiting for the sun to brighten the day. He washed his dishes and stepped out the door. Just as he opened it, the wooden frame exploded next to his head, sending splinters into his cheek and neck.

Instinct took over—Dan fell backward into the house as more bullets pinged into the walls inside and out. Cursing loudly, he low crawled across the living room toward Ben's gun cabinet. Reaching inside, he pulled out the first rifle he touched—a Korean War-era M1 Garand Carbine. Fishing around, he found a couple of magazines in a drawer that fit. He crawled back to the door and peeked around the edge. The firing had stopped, but as soon as the attackers saw movement, they resumed their assault.

Dan loaded the carbine and pushed the barrel through the door. He spotted one shooter behind the corral directly across the yard from the house, his rifle sticking through the fence. A second attacker was stationed at the corner of the fence outside the corral. Dan took aim at the first man and fired off three rounds in quick succession. Wood chips flew from the fence, and the shooter's rifle shot up into the air as he fell backward.

The second shooter, seeing his partner down, turned and began running down the driveway. Dan again took aim and fired once. The runner dropped his rifle, staggered a few steps, and fell face-first into the gravel road, skidding a few feet. A small round hole between his shoulder blades.

With no more immediate threat, Dan leaned the carbine against the wall and went into the bathroom. Looking in the mirror, his face resembled a porcupine with slivers of wood stuck to his skin. Blood dribbled down his neck. Gritting his teeth, he began pulling out the worst of the splinters. Then, he wrapped his face and neck in a wet towel and headed out to his truck. He needed to call the authorities and get an ambulance.

As Ben approached his yard, he saw two sheriff's deputy cars and an ambulance. "What the hell?" Ben asked himself. When he got out of his truck, he saw Dan sitting on the steps of the porch, an attendant working on his face. A deputy stood nearby.

"What the hell goes on here?" Ben asked as he walked up.

Through gritted teeth, Dan looked up and said, "Damn Mexican cartel started shooting this morning for breakfast."

The ambulance attendant shook his head without looking up. "They weren't Mexican," he said. "They looked like Arabs."

Ben stood there for a moment, then said, "Could they be Iranians?"

"Could be. They had no identification on them," the medic replied as he pulled another splinter from Dan's neck, causing him to wince.

"Then this is my fault, Dan. They thought you were me. I'm sorry," Ben said, shaking his head.

"Well, the sons of bitches won't make that mistake again. But in the long run, I get more work out of you. Someone's gonna have to fix this house up." Dan grinned at Ben.

Chapter Eleven

Ben spent the next half hour explaining to the deputy why the attack was a mistake by the Taliban and why they were after him. He didn't delve into the specifics of what he had done to the Taliban. The deputy finally said the only thing questionable about the affair was the fact that the second gunman was shot in the back. He was looking directly at Dan when he said it.

"Hell, he had been shooting at me! You don't think I was gonna let him get away to come back later, do you?" Dan growled at the deputy.

The deputy nodded and said it made sense to him. He closed his notebook and turned to leave but stopped and said, "Do you all want a security guard here? I can request one if you think this isn't the end."

Ben shook his head. "These guys are smart, and we can't live under security forever. We'll be fine. Maybe send a car out once a day to check how things are next time."

Dan giggled at that.

When the cars and the ambulance had left and the dust settled, Ben went inside and came back out with two cold beers. Handing one to Dan, he said, "I'm sorry about this. I didn't think they would figure out so quickly where I was."

"You don't think they might have had some help in that, do you?" Dan asked as he swallowed a healthy slug of beer.

"What do you mean? There's only a handful of people who know what I'm doing and where I am," Ben answered.

"Well, one of them could have spilled the beans, maybe not directly, but where someone else could've heard it. Don't ya think that's possible?" Dan almost drained the bottle.

"I guess, but those guys came in here during the night with no opposition. Maybe we need a dog or two. Real noise makers." Ben was thinking out loud.

"Hey, that's a good idea, and I know where they might be. There's an old lady in town who has a neighbor who has two barking mutts. Every time she has company, those dogs raise hell. I think the owner would be happy to get them gone to a good home because they've been known to bite." Dan explained.

"Sounds like you have firsthand knowledge of these dogs. Did they bite you?" Ben was laughing.

"That don't matter, they bite, and if those diaper heads come back, we will know it." Dan growled.

"What do you mean, we? Haven't you already had enough of my mess? You got my money, isn't that, and this, enough?" Ben looked him square in the eye.

"I don't want someone else being hurt because of my grudge match with these people," Dan said firmly.

"Hey, I took the heat, and that puts me in, like it or not. I don't want your money, well, not much. I gotta fix up this house, but you can't stay here alone. The more people here, the better chance of sending the alarm when the bad guys show up. Like it or not, I'm in. If you won't let me stay here, I'll put my tent down by the road. These guys just can't shoot up a man and get away with it!" Dan was mad.

"Okay, Okay, but don't say I didn't warn ya," Ben cautioned.

Chapter Twelve

The next morning, Dan drove into the yard just at sunup. In the back of his truck were two matching brindle dogs. They had the head and forelimbs of a pit bull but the body and back legs of a hound. Dan got out and walked over to Ben, who was standing on the porch with a cup of coffee.

"Well, Boss, there they are."

"I thought they bit; how did you get them?" Ben asked.

"I fed them a ball of hamburger, and while they were eating it, I snapped the chain on their collars." Dan was grinning.

"And what did you have to do to get them?" Ben asked.

"I fed them a ball of hamburger and snapped the chain on them," Dan growled.

"In other words, you stole two dogs?" Ben tossed out the dregs of his coffee.

"Well, they ain't gonna bark at me when I go see Vera anymore. I even know their names. That one there is Ketchem and the other one is Killum; see, ranch security at its best. I'll chain them down at the barn for now." Dan walked to his truck, and Ben went back into the house.

Later that day, Ben was in town getting supplies and fuel for his truck. As he walked out the door at the filling station, he noticed a soldier sitting on the sidewalk with his back to the wall. His knees were drawn up, his arms crossed and resting on the knees, his head bowed down resting on his arms. He wore camouflaged fatigues with a ball cap pulled down to cover his eyes. A backpack lay beside him.

Ben walked over and nudged him with his boot. "Hey." He said. The sleeping soldier raised his head and looked up with the bluest eyes Ben had ever seen.

When Ben realized this soldier was a woman, he took a step back. "You look give out; can I help you?" he asked.

"Just what kind of help you got in mind?" She answered.

"Well, a meal and a place to rest; then a ride to wherever you're going. That's all. I'm a vet too. I just want to help." Ben answered.

"I have been hitching it for three days, I'm out 'a cash and I'm beat. So, I guess if that's all you want to do, I'll go along with it. I was just discharged on the west coast, and I'm headed east." She struggled to stand up, and Ben picked up the backpack, then showed her where the truck was.

On the way to the ranch, he explained where he lived and that when she was rested, he would take her to Casa Grande and stake her to a bus ticket to wherever she was going. At the house, Dan was on a ladder patching a bullet hole in the wall. As Ben escorted the girl into the house, Dan asked:

"Did you tell her? You better tell her."

"She's just here for the night, then I'll take her to a bus. But I'll tell her anyway," Ben said.

Dan nodded and went back to work. Inside the house, Ben showed the girl the bathroom, then where the extra bed was and told her who Dan was.

"I'll start supper here in a bit. If you want a cold drink, help yourself. I'll be outside doing chores." He stepped out the screen door.

"What the hell are you doing?" Dan asked from up on the ladder.

"Just trying to help a fellow soldier and vet out, that's down on her luck," Ben answered.

"Well, that could get you in some kind of trouble." Dan mused.

"I been in trouble before." Was all that Ben said.

Chapter Thirteen

When Ben and Dan started toward the house later that afternoon, a tantalizing aroma wafted out the screen door. As they stepped into the house, the sight they found stopped them dead in their tracks. The table was set, and bowls of hot food were spread around. Vegetables, gravy, and fried steak. Their newfound boarder was dressed in a clean olive drab tee shirt and jeans. Her hair was still damp but brushed out, hanging down to her shoulders.

While not a movie star, Ben found her full figure and blue eyes an attractive sight. Dan brushed by Ben and slid into a chair, loading his plate.

"Fellas, my name is Gloria Hayes, folks just call me Glory. I figured since I got a shower and a fresh bed, I could trade it out with a home-cooked meal." She pulled the blonde hair back away from her face.

Ben still stood there in shock. Dan looked up with his mouth full and said, "You better get to it, Ben; this is way better than the greasy spoon vittles you fix."

Ben pulled out a chair for Glory and seated her, then pulled his chair closer to the table.

"Dan, where's your manners?"

"Ain't got any when it comes to food this good," Dan said between bites.

"I better tell you something, Glory." Ben started in.

"What, that you were targeted by some Iranians? That you expect more? Well, you better listen to what I have to say first. You see, I'm not freshly discharged from the Army. I've been out a couple of years, and like you, I went to work for a different group. I'm now with homeland security, undercover. I was sent here when we got word of the attack on the ranch. If they do it again, I'm to get a live prisoner."

She looked at Dan, who had a shocked and sheepish look on his face.

"We don't believe the attack was in response to the wanted poster. It's something more. We have been monitoring a cartel group in Caborca, Mexico. During the winter months, they send a lot of mules up here with contraband. We can watch them through the Papago Reservation, but when they get here, they disappear. My job is to find where they go, but I'll need your help. I need to survey the southern border of the ranch. I know in the summer months there won't be any mules moving, too hot, so we have three months or so to figure out where the mules go to. Plus, I don't think they will try to get you again. But when it cools off, they will want you gone. We think that's what the firefight was about, and somebody tipped them off to your being here."

Glory filled her plate when she finished.

"I know you have a lot of questions, but the food is getting cold." Ben had sat back in his chair, stupefied.

"You mean to tell me that picking you up was a set-up?"

"Yep, but you made it easier than we thought it would be," Glory said, slicing a piece of steak and forked it into her mouth.

"This is good beef, some of yours?" Ben nodded as he started filling his plate.

"Looks like we'll need to butcher another one too."

Chapter Fourteen

The next morning, Ben was at the barn saddling horses in the gray dawn. It had been a hot, sweltering night, and the day promised to be worse. He wanted an early start. Dan was going to town to pick up a swamp cooler for the house and find the brand inspector. The brands on the corral full of mavericks were starting to peel. If he would inspect them, Ben wanted to send them to the sale barn.

Glory came strolling to the barn just as Ben was loading the horses into the trailer. He planned to haul to the gun-site well, which was about halfway along the south fence line. He thought it would take three or four days to ride the whole line. By hauling the horses as close as possible, they would save many hot, long rides. Glory jumped in the cab of the truck, and they rolled out of the yard.

"You ride, do you?" Ben asked.

"Yes, I've ridden since I was a little girl, why?" she answered.

"Well, a tee shirt and shorts isn't exactly the type of clothes to wear here. First, you will sunburn like a biscuit, second, everything in the desert will either scratch, or stick, or stab. I'd hate to see those pretty legs all scarred up," Ben said.

"I'll be okay. I think I know what to wear," Glory was a little miffed.

Ben nodded, but said no more. When they pulled into the area at gun-site well, a handful of cows were leaving the corral after having watered. Ben just sat behind the wheel watching them.

"They don't look too wild, do they?" Glory asked.

"No, that's why I wonder if any cattle were shipped off this ranch by the bank. These cattle aren't afraid of trucks or men on horseback. We haven't chased them either. We just trap them with those triggers you see there." Ben pointed out the set triggers built into the corral fence.

"I wonder if an audit of the bank records would tell us anything?" Glory asked.

"It wouldn't hurt, but in the meantime, let's make some tracks. It's gonna get hot as the hinges on hell's doors," Ben jumped out. After unloading the horses, he hung a canvas water bag on his saddle horn.

"We really need that?" Glory asked.

"Yep, it's a long way we've got to ride, and you are going to get thirsty as well as full of stickers," Ben answered.

"I can go a long way without a drink." Glory lifted her chin in defiance.

"Well, just so you know, I might want a drink along the way, but I wouldn't force it on you," Ben snickered.

Later that afternoon, they were back at the trailer, the canvas water bag now flopped empty on the saddle horn. Glory's face, arms, and legs were burned red, and they had stopped a couple of times to remove thorns from her legs. Ben had refrained from saying, "I told you so."

Glory painfully slid out of the saddle, and when she hit the ground, her knees buckled. Ben caught her. She looked up at Ben and half smiled.

"This isn't anything like a show ring in Maryland," she said.

"No, ma'am, we'll be better prepared next time though." Ben opened the truck door and helped her in the passenger side. He loaded the horses and turned for home when he started the truck. In his mind, he didn't think they would be back for a couple of days.

At the ranch, Dan was putting the finishing touches on the evaporative cooler. He had positioned it in a window of the house to blow down the hallway. By cracking a window in each bedroom, it would draw the cool air through. He had run into Cliff in town and explained about the brand inspector but hadn't mentioned Glory. While he liked Cliff, Dan wasn't completely sold on him.

An hour before dark, Ben and Glory drove into the yard. Their dust hadn't settled when the brand inspector pulled up. Glory hobbled to the house while Ben and the inspector looked at the cattle.

"New girlfriend?" the inspector asked as Glory went into the house.

"Housekeeper. Dan don't like my cooking," was all Ben said.

"Mmm, looks like you took her for a hard ride."

"Well, she asked for it," Ben turned a steer around for the brand inspector.

Dan was sitting on the fence watching them. He slowly got down and went to the house where he started the cooler running. The solar panels would just barely keep up with the electrical drain, but the house cooled down from the day's heat. Summers in Gila Bend could be brutal.

Chapter Fifteen

Two mornings after the inspector wrote out the papers on the cattle, Ben loaded them on a cattle truck. He handed the envelope to the driver. **Marana Stockyard** was written on it. Dan was in the barn working on a project of some kind. As Ben rode to the house, he saw a red and sunburned face peering out the window. He ducked his head and rode on.

Glory had been in misery since coming back from the first ride along the south fence. Dan had gone out and cut some aloe vera leaves and squeezed the juice out to rub on the worst of the sunburns.

No sooner had Ben stepped down from his horse than a deputy's car rolled into the yard.

"You Ben Kool?" he asked.

Ben nodded and said, "What can I do for you?"

"You know a cowpuncher desert rat named Cliff?" he asked.

"Yeah, why?"

"Well, he wanted me to bring you a message, he's laid up in town, he said 'to watch out, they are back'."

The deputy was shaking his head. "He said you knew what he was talking about."

Dan had walked up behind Ben just as the deputy finished. Ben turned to him, "I guess you heard that?"

"Yeah, just what I wanted to hear on a good morning like today." Dan grumbled.

"Where is Cliff?" Ben asked.

"The hospital with a broken leg. He said a horse fell on him."

The deputy had started toward his car. "Thanks, I'll go check on him," was all Ben said.

A few hours later, Ben was standing by Cliff's bedside. Cliff's leg was in a cast from crotch to ankle. His eyes were droopy from the painkillers, but he recognized Ben.

"You better keep a close eye on the south fence line. Those mules might show up. Also, they are armed now. That horse just didn't fall on me, he was shot out from under me. I had to crawl a quarter mile to my truck to get here," Cliff gritted his teeth.

"What about your outfit? Someone need to go take care of things?" Ben asked.

"No, the Morales brothers will. I don't think the Caborca Cartel will mess with them, being they are Mexican. I had fixed a hole in my fence when the trash shot ole Baldy. I heard them jabbering out in the brush, they were Mexican for sure. They thought they had killed me. They can't shoot for sour apples. Poor ole Baldy took the hit."

Cliff was fading but trying to stay awake.

"Your place is next. I don't know what's so damned important for them to trek through the desert this time of year, but it is important. Keep a sharp eye out to the south," he said.

Ben nodded and asked if he needed something brought to him, but Cliff was snoring.

Ben went out in the hallway and ran into the deputy.

"Does this have to do with the shootout at your place a while back?" he asked.

"It has everything to do with it; I'm sorry ole Cliff got hammered with it," Ben replied.

"Do you need some help? We can be out there for as long as you need," offered the deputy.

"No, because I don't know when or where they will come up, but you might let the Border Patrol know what's up, or at least send them out to the ranch," Ben answered.

He turned to leave, then stopped and thanked the deputy, "I gotta get home, Dan is out there by himself."

"Well, it will be bad for the Mexicans if they are after what happened to those Iranians," the deputy smiled.

Ben left the hospital parking lot with squealing tires. "We need a live one," was what he thought to himself.

Chapter Sixteen

All was quiet at the ranch when Ben got back. Dan met him in the yard, asking how Cliff was.

"He's going to be okay in six weeks or so. Do you think Ketchem and Killum can be turned loose? We may need a patrol at night," Ben asked.

"I'll turn them loose. I hope one of us doesn't get bit," Dan grumbled.

The next morning, in the dark, Ben was saddling horses and loading them in his trailer. The dogs stood a few feet away watching. From the house, Glory came across the yard. She had borrowed a pair of Dan's Levi's and a long-sleeved shirt. Ben had presented her with an old straw hat he had saved. In her right hand, she carried the M1 Garand Carbine.

"What's Dan gonna use while you got his shooter?" Ben asked.

"He told me to take it. He has a .223 he's going to use. I just hope we don't need these," Glory said as she got into the truck.

A few moments later, the truck left the yard in a cloud of dust with the two dogs barking at the wheels.

Dan was watching from the shop door and called the dogs back. His .223 Savage was leaning against the wall just inside. He picked it up and started toward the house.

"You dogs keep an eye for the chili varmints," was all he said.

When Ben and Glory arrived at the gunsight corrals, they found a six-inch stream of water running through the corral. The float on the water trough had been removed and the water was free flowing from the storage tank. Ben jumped out, ran into the corral, and was putting the float back on the pipe. Glory was out walking around the corral peering down at the ground.

"Here they go!" she yelled at Ben when she found the trail of footprints. When Ben had the float fixed, he went to the trailer and unloaded the horses, all the while cussing under his breath.

"It takes a week to fill that storage. We lost about half of it, I figure. Dirty sons, in this country you can't waste water."

Putting the rifles in the saddle holsters, they mounted and struck a long trot on the trail of footprints left by the mules. Ben thought they couldn't be much over an hour ahead. In actuality, they were shaded up just two miles from the corrals.

The four mules were scattered in a small mesquite thicket, thinking they were safe until dark. They had no idea that the trail they left was leading Ben and Glory straight to them. Julio was the youngest of the four mules. He couldn't seem to rest; he was always moving and squirreling around. He got up and walked to the edge of the thicket, looking back at the way he had come. In his backpack was cocaine wrapped in plastic wrap. His .30-30 rifle lay under the mesquite where he had tried to catch a nap.

Out across the desert, he saw a plume of dust approaching. He turned and yelled at the other three mules. Instantly, they were on their feet and by his side. Each mule carried a long gun of some sort. Without a spoken word, they scattered in four different directions, taking their packs and rifles, they silently drifted away.

When Ben and Glory trotted up on the thicket, they found a mess of footprints going every which way. They rode in opposite directions around the thicket. Meeting on the back side.

"They split, not too long ago. It's follow one or none," Ben said.

"If we follow one, we may find their meeting place along the way, but I want to know where they came in here," Glory said as she gritted her teeth.

"Let's backtrack them, maybe we can get a feel for what they are doing," she continued.

"I hate letting these guys get away and I don't want to split up. I hope the Border Patrol finds them," Ben said as he reined his horse around and started back.

If Ben and Glory had gone any further, they would have been met with rifle fire from the leader of the mules. Antonio was a known killer in Mexico; he liked the thrill and adrenaline rush. He was waiting just a scant half mile ahead when he saw the riders turn back. He uncocked the rifle he held. The drop-off point for the contraband they carried was just a little way farther, then they could start back. He hoped this was the last load this season, it was getting hot!

At the corral, it didn't take long to find the trail of the mules where they came to the corral. A small piece of camo cloth was snagged on a mesquite bush. With heads down, they started following the trail back to the southwest. A few hours later, they came to the south boundary fence. The mules had cut the fence, then spliced it back, making a small gate by tying the wires together with a smooth wire. It would turn the cattle if one didn't push against it, but it could easily be opened to walk through. Ben got off his horse to mend it back right, but Glory stopped him.

"They will just cut it again. Leave it! Now we know where they are coming in, we can watch this spot for them to cross. We won't have to ride the whole fence line to find them."

Ben nodded in agreement.

"If we have time, let's go see where they went."

They turned their horses back the way they had come.

Chapter Seventeen

Julio stumbled as his ankle twisted in a hole in the sandy soil. The weight of his backpack pinned him down as he fell heavily to the ground. A shadow loomed over him, and Antonio stood there, looking down with cold determination.

"Give me the pack," Antonio said, holding out his hand.

"Help me up. I can finish," Julio pleaded, though deep down, he knew he couldn't. The pain in his ankle felt like fire, and every attempt to push himself up was futile.

"Give me the pack," Antonio repeated, his tone firm. Julio, knowing there would be no return, slipped his arms from the shoulder straps and handed the pack to Antonio.

"Will you leave me some water?" Julio asked softly.

Antonio took the pack without a word and walked away.

The bankers Anderson and Caldwell orchestrated a vast drug network, with dealers distributing the product while never touching the drugs themselves. Once a week, these dealers visited the bank and deposited cash into a numbered account. The bankers then transferred the money offshore.

The weakest link was their pickup man in Gila Bend, a known prescription drug user always short on cash despite weekly payments. They feared he might eventually steal a load of contraband. Antonio, aware of this weakness, wanted to become that driver—his chance to stay in the United States.

The pickup point was an abandoned World War II ammunition depot near a remote rail line in southern Arizona. Few locals were aware of its existence. From a distance, it resembled a sandy mound.

When Antonio arrived at the depot, the driver sat in the shade, smoking cigarette after cigarette. The three mules—Antonio's associates—loaded the packs into the back seat of the car. Antonio then pulled a wad of cash from his pocket and handed a portion to each mule. They turned back toward Mexico.

Antonio looked at the driver, his long brown greasy hair partially covering his face. "Get out!" he commanded.

"Why?" the driver asked, puzzled.

Antonio responded by shooting him in the face. After pulling the lifeless body from the car, Antonio wiped the blood from the interior as best he could. He then dragged the corpse behind the rounded mound of the depot and left it there.

Getting into the car, Antonio drove off toward Phoenix and his new life.

Back in the desert, Julio struggled to find a way to make it back to the gun-site corral. As the sun set behind the Telegraph Hills, two riders approached.

"There's your live one," Ben said to Glory, glancing at Julio.

With a look of a cornered animal, Julio didn't speak English but saw a glimmer of hope in these two. At least he wouldn't die here alone.

Ben explained in broken Mexican that Julio was to ride behind Glory. After securing him onto her horse, they headed back toward the truck.

Along the ride, Ben questioned Julio about his involvement in the smuggling operation. It became clear that Julio was a novice—this was his first trip to Arizona. He knew little beyond Antonio and his brutal tactics.

Julio shared the pickup spot at the abandoned ammunition storage facility near the rail tracks. Antonio, he explained, used and discarded those who couldn't complete their tasks. Promised a big payday, Julio had little hope of receiving payment now.

That evening, Ben and Glory delivered Julio to the Border Patrol in Gila Bend.

"Well, we didn't get much out of him, but at least we know more than we did before," Glory said as she watched the Border Patrol paddy wagon drive away. "Still feels kind of helpless, especially knowing there's a psycho killer hauling those drugs."

Ben only nodded in agreement. "Let's go, I'm hungry. Been a long day."

Chapter Eighteen

Antonio stepped through the double glass doors of the Salt River National Bank. He wore a silk white sports shirt and black cotton slacks with razor-sharp creases down each leg. His hair was slicked back, and his polished shoes sparkled with a new shine.

He walked straight to Jimmy Caldwell and stood before his desk. "I need to see Mister Anderson," was all he said. Caldwell looked up, a chill running down his spine.

"I'll check and see if he is available," Caldwell said as he slid his chair back and stepped toward the door behind him.

Before Caldwell could even open the door, Antonio pushed past him and walked up to the banker's desk. "My name is Antonio Varga. I'm your new driver."

Anderson slowly lifted his gaze to meet the man before him. A shiver ran down his spine. "I don't have a chauffeur."

"No, I drive between Gila Bend and South Phoenix," Antonio said, his voice calm and unwavering.

"What happened to my driver?" Anderson asked, his voice tight with concern.

"He quit. I'm taking his place. I have a message for you from the cartel. From now on, they will send a shipment once a week, year-round. You need to be prepared to liquidate the contraband weekly, instead of monthly," Antonio said with a cold smile—like a rattlesnake ready to strike.

Anderson leaned back in his chair, eyes narrowing. "I don't know, this is short notice. We can try, but bringing the mules up weekly will raise suspicion. We had to sell the Conley Ranch, and the new owner is always around."

"I can take care of the problem," Antonio replied smoothly.

Pulling a sheet of paper from his desk, Anderson slid it across the desk toward Antonio. "This is the man. You eliminate him, and I'll double the reward."

Anderson reached into his desk and removed an envelope, handing it to Antonio. Inside, there was an ATM card along with a card bearing his private phone number. "Call me from now on. Don't come here. We'll deposit your weekly pay to the account linked to that card. Every Monday, draw on it."

Anderson's discomfort was palpable.

Antonio stood and turned toward the door. As he walked away, Anderson watched him all the way out, his mind racing.

Turning back to Caldwell, Anderson said, "I think we might better consider retirement. Even if he gets Ben Kool, we'll still have to deal with the cartel. We've got plenty stashed, and we might want to move to South America."

Caldwell nodded. "That guy will be a loose cannon for sure. When do we go?"

"At week's end, when we close for the weekend. It will give us two days to make our departure. Make sure everything is transferred and get reservations to a country with no extradition. No slip-ups now," Anderson said firmly.

Chapter Nineteen

The road to the Conley ranch house and headquarters stretched for two miles of dirt. It had one destination—no turn-offs or side roads. Just one road all the way. Antonio had driven about halfway down the path and then pulled over. The highway was out of sight behind him, and the house wasn't yet in view.

Raising the hood of the car, Antonio placed a 9mm Glock on the engine air cleaner on the driver's side. Then, he waited. It wasn't long.

Ben Kool's faded blue Dodge Power Wagon appeared in the distance. Antonio kept his head down under the hood, as though inspecting the engine. His right hand rested on the Glock.

He heard a door slam and peered around the car to see Ben walking toward him. "Need a hand?" Ben said, his voice steady, when Glory's voice rang out from the other side of the car. "GUN!"

Antonio whipped the Glock around the hood, raising it to bear on Ben. However, before he could pull the trigger, Ben had already dropped to the ground.

At the same moment, Antonio began spinning in a half-circle, as the sharp crack of three quick shots rang out. Antonio dead-weight fell onto the dirt, first to his knees and then onto his back as blood pumped from one hole in his throat and two in his chest.

Ben got up, walking toward the downed gunman, his movements steady, the only sounds now an engine running and steps on the ground. Glory was soon standing to one side, her pistol still in hand. Antonio's blazing eyes locked onto Ben. He opened his mouth to speak, but it filled with blood, which oozed from the corners. His gaze dulled, and he was finished.

Glory walked over and holstered her pistol, pulling a handkerchief from her hip pocket. "Here, stand still," she said, dabbing at the blood dribbling from Ben's ear lobe.

"He damn near got you good; you know this guy?" she asked.

"Never saw him before in my life. Let's see if he has any ID," Ben replied, wiping away the remaining blood.

After rifling through the dead man's pockets, they found only a debit card and a business card for Anderson at the bank.

"Well, that explains a lot," Glory said, her tone thoughtful.

"I'll take the truck and go get a deputy and the Border Patrol. What you wanna bet this guy is illegal?" Glory asked, her expression grim.

Ben shook his head. "No bet, but don't mention the debit card or Anderson's card until we have time to think this through."

Glory nodded and climbed into the Dodge truck. She was back within an hour, accompanied by a deputy and an ambulance.

The deputy approached the scene, staring down at the corpse. "This is getting to be a routine trip out here, Ben. Any idea who this one is?"

Ben shook his head, his jaw tightening.

The ambulance attendant moved to Ben, who still held a handkerchief to his ear. The attendant pulled the hand away and examined the ear. "Well, sir, you won't have a place for an earring on this side anymore, but I think pirates only wear one earring anyway."

"Funny boy," Ben muttered, his voice sharp as the EMT led him to the back of the ambulance.

Ben, now bandaged with a fresh dressing on his ear, sat in the truck on the passenger side, watching the EMT load Antonio's lifeless body into the ambulance.

Glory was speaking with the deputy, waving her hands about as she explained the situation. Eventually, she returned to the truck and slid behind the wheel.

"We gotta head back to town to file the report. Barney Fife over there says with a questionable shooting…" her voice trailed off as the deputy walked by on his way to his car.

"I didn't think there was anything questionable about it. He shot first, and you shot second. Unless they think the second and third shots weren't needed," Ben growled.

Glory started the truck and followed the deputy back to town, the dusty road disappearing behind them.

Chapter Twenty

Ben Kool stood outside the sheriff's office in the dark. Inside, he could hear Glory raising her voice at the deputy. He was in a foul mood. After returning home to escape violence and chaos, here he was neck-deep in it again. The thought of walking away was tempting, but he knew he was committed to too many people. They were counting on him to untangle this mess.

When Glory finally walked out, her head was bowed, focused on the sidewalk.

"You hurting?" she asked softly.

"No, just thinking about the mess I've dragged everyone into," Ben mumbled. "I never thought it would turn out like this."

"You didn't get anyone into any mess," Glory said firmly. "Hell, I'm here doing my job. I would've done it with you or without. This is just the way it turned out."

She paused, then asked, "Do you know about an old ammo dump along the train tracks?"

"Yeah, it's east of here. Really, I guess it's on the ranch. We used to go party there in high school. Why?" Ben answered.

"The track crew found a dead man there this morning. Shot in the face. That's what me and Barney in there were arguing about," Glory said, gesturing toward the deputy inside. "He thinks one of us did it."

"Well, ain't he the smart one. I think he just likes having you around," Ben smiled.

"Well, it won't do him any good. I've got my eyes on something better. Can we go to that dump in the morning? I'd like to check it out," Glory asked.

"Sure. First thing at sunup, before it gets too hot," Ben replied.

They climbed into the truck, and Ben drove them home. After a short time, he said, "Let's go get some shut eye."

The next morning, Ben and Glory walked around the ammo dump. They found where the corpse had been lying and saw the drag marks leading from where it had been shot.

Ben saw nothing of use here, but Glory continued her search until a deputy drove up.

"I got word on something you all might find interesting," he said, walking toward them. "Phoenix police found two dead guys in a car parked in an alley. Shot in the back of the head. One bullet each. Names were Caldwell and Anderson. A bunch of bank records were found in a briefcase with Anderson."

"Would you know anything about that?"

"Now why would we know about it? Those are the guys who handled the sale of the ranch for me when I bought it from the bank," Ben said, his irritation evident.

"That sounds like an old-time mob hit," the deputy murmured, nodding slightly before heading back to his car.

Glory walked up as the deputy started the engine.

"Damn guy following us?" she asked.

"No, just keeping his eye on you, I think," Ben snickered.

Glory grunted in response.

Ben headed the Dodge back toward the ranch, raising a cloud of dust behind him. When they pulled into the ranch yard, another battle scene awaited them.

One of the Morales boys lay across the steps to the porch. Dan was sprawled face down on the porch, an M1 carbine beside him.

Ben rushed up and gently rolled Dan over onto his back. Dan's eyes fluttered open.

"I g-g-got one," he said weakly. "I think the other has some lead in him, but he's still around. Be careful."

"What the hell happened?" Ben asked sharply.

"They work for the cartel. They're cleaning up everyone who was with the bank. I was the last one," Dan whispered before fading fast.

"You work for the bank?" Ben asked, his voice rising.

"Yep. They paid too well. I couldn't pass it up," Dan whispered just before exhaling a final breath.

Ben gently laid his head back on the porch floor.

Glory was standing at the foot of the porch steps when a pop sounded, and she fell to the ground, clutching her leg and cursing loudly.

"It came from the barn!" she yelled.

Ben jumped into a run, zigzagging across the yard as bullets kicked up dust where he had been mere seconds before.

When he burst through the barn door, Jaime Morales lay slumped against the wall. Seeing Ben, Jaime raised his pistol, but Ben quickly fired two rounds into his chest.

Jaime slumped to the ground, and Ben walked over to take the pistol from his hand. The magazine was empty.

"DAMN!" Ben said, frustration clear, as he turned back toward the door.

At the porch, Glory was holding a piece of her shirt tail over the wound in her thigh.

Ben picked her up and carried her to the truck.

"I gotta get you to a doctor. I guess it's my turn to take care of you," he said as he slammed the door.

"Do we have to see that damned deputy again?" Glory asked quietly as they pulled out of the yard.

Chapter Twenty-one

Ben made sure that Glory was going to be okay at the hospital. She grumbled about being left there, but the doctors insisted she stay at least 24 hours. After alerting the sheriff, the deputy, and an ambulance about the shootout at the ranch, Ben led them back.

While the ambulance attendants were body bagging the Morales brothers, Ben discovered the dogs, Ketchem and Killum, chained behind the barn. He released them, and they promptly attempted to bite the deputy.

Later, as the deputy and ambulance left, Ben poured himself a glass of whiskey and settled onto the creaky porch steps. The warm, dry desert air wrapped around him, the faint scent of sagebrush and mesquite carried on the breeze. His hands trembled slightly as he brought the glass to his lips, the familiar burn of the whiskey a comfort in the quiet aftermath of violence.

The sun dipped low on the horizon, casting long shadows over the ranch yard, while the soft hum of cicadas filled the still evening air. The faint rustling of the dogs' fur against the wooden planks beneath his feet was the only sound, except for the distant croak of a lone raven perched on a fencepost.

Ben closed his eyes for a moment, allowing the weight of the past few days to settle in. Memories of Rattlesnake Dan, Glory's resilience, and the harsh realities of life on the ranch flooded his thoughts. A sense of peace began to creep in, though the ghosts of those lost still lingered in the corners of his mind.

When he returned the next day for Glory, he found she had been on the phone with her contacts at Homeland Security. The federales in Caborca had raided the cartel there. A shootout had ensued, and the cartel leaders were dead. Finally, he could draw a long breath.

In the Gila Bend cemetery, in a far corner at the head of a fresh grave with a few flowers scattered over it. It has a marble headstone on which is the simple engraving:

RATTLESNAKE DAN
Vietnam Veteran